THE BOOK OF ARMOUR

GHOSTWRITER
Copyright © 2022 GHOSTWRITER
All rights reserved.
ISBN: 9798355215682
Instagram: @Ghostwriter_ig

CHOOSE YOUR CHARACTER

Choose your CHARACTER

Put on your ARMOUR

Press start to PLAY

For there's only one way to gain, a leverage from a world of pain.

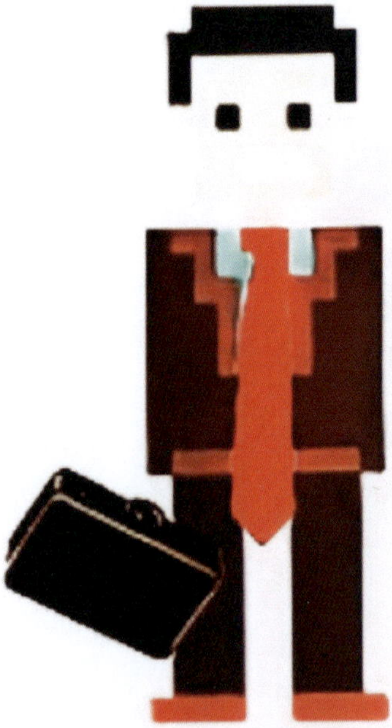

THE STATUS MAN

*T*he status man is a very proud man,
a very honourable man
he conducts his morality
with principles that he has set,
developed his own defence
a character he invents.
Three children a wife in spirit,
a home he barely visits
for a weakness he knows or does not
thou he strides for tomorrow to banish the rot.
A core strength of armour he lords
hurt by ways
The Status Man craves
the attention
but not emotionally fazed,
ousted by the fear
of the olden days.
A man from nothing,
reputation his everything
growing up in humble living conditions
working his way to the top was his only way to fight,
to stop the rot.

The Book Of Armour

A bedsit accommodation
troublesome mitigation
dreams were adlibbed
No job
No family
No bargaining chip,
only one passion and that was to make it big.
Driven by the shadowy shreds that live inside his containership
this was his goal and his aspiration
nothing else mattered…
The hard comings of life he never imagined.
A man from nothing
planning and envisioning
his reputation imprisoning,
in the hope to dispose humble living conditioning.
A neglected child appears from the reckoning
a hard life beckoning
for a vulnerable adolescent
that needed weaponing.
Dreams and goals of Jaguars
double garages and jewellery of gold,
these were the ingredients
he believed he needed for his past to be sold.

Status became ever so important to him
his life gradually started to get better
a new hymn
a new meaning, it brought him reasoning,
he called it; "the epitome of ultimate living."

The Book Of Armour

A solidarity lies his pride and treasure
without measure
he weathered the weather.
A heart and armour can never combine
conscience severed
steel and leather leaves a heart behind,
his emotions hidden and tethered.
a man obsessed with what he wants to gain and forget
possessions are a compromise he shoulders the debt
a man of vent didn't dither or take a second to regret.
Only had time for his aesthetic care,
a life so bare
one thing that held an importance,
was an unwanted nostalgia
a past life that to him was painfully unfair.
A promotion is his motivation
a love he can't kiss
the only thing that made him whole
is the dream of being on Forbes rich list.

A name badge, a sum
for a 9 to 5, a man succumbs
as it's the only way for the machine to run.
Life is created by the mind
an illusion, a way for the walking blind.
Time is precious but a Status Man knows know different
he's just trying to get through
a better life less plausible
his armour got bulkier, heavier less durable
for a status unexplainable.

The Book Of Armour

A substantial investment
a man who truly believes
the unattainable is attainable
his ego was unleashed.
He floated his soul he has sold his stocks
secretly drowning while he worked around the clock.
He moved on from his bedsit home
Cornflakes had turned to big breakfast midday lunches,
Ford Cortina's to Jaguar XJS's
Oh, how the heart is only credited by the crunches.

A middle-class girl
a bus stop she sat
a brown fur coat
fingers through her hair
as it looked a little flat.
Her cigarette was out
as a match caught alight,
a date at a time
a lady constructed of what he designed.

A status had come together through their hidden pain
septic by infection, a manifested mistake,
morals and a loving nature flushed down the drain
all for a life that hid what he obtained.
A believable illusion he had to create
in order to defeat life's attack and array.

So, he got himself a new soul mate
to feed what he had to taint
his status gathered pace
a self-made delusional state,
she became his slave what he asked for, she gave.

As the power was super, so was her name
a marriage made in heaven or two people in need of aid
the truth is not adhered for two people bowed to their own individual fear
for having no armour, self-esteem disappears.
A baby bloomed, this lady now has a roof
for now she's happy as Larry
for he had a gap in the front tooth.
A girl built to live under somebody's half-truth,
for a status man this wasn't the way forward
still a void, a man with a need to fill the void
he had a hunch and worked till his back broke
living for a status, emotion he had no choice to duck.
He couldn't give love
he didn't like to be touched
especially from the heart,
a soldier at war fighting for his craft.
His bank took account for the overdraft
all for an image, his peers thought were clean cut.
Investment moves but emotions heeled by the hoof
a lady patiently waiting for a loving home, she hopes may loom
but in reality she sits at home a house wife 40 Marlboro's.

The Book Of Armour

A shot of Smirnoff to awake the nerve
morning television all alone
his thoughts were not with her
a man trying to get through,
both hibernating in two different rooms.
Both afraid but battling with two different moves
a mechanism built but hurt concludes,
two people not realising why they do the things they do
arguments formed from misunderstanding that feuds
it paves way for people to be used.
The love they both desire still eludes
misguided by earths movements the ego blew
a core strength an atmospheric doom
for people that live together
who will never suit.

A self-made millionaire but the cupboards were bare
far too self-consumed with a status to heal a wound.
One bad-mouthing another a vice that grew,
for his beloved, a signal not tuned
like a radar trying to hear back from the moon.
All hell has broken cupid's promise was loose
O how the misery had turned the hopeful mood.
Self-inflicted by an overspilt cup, words hidden that live in the gut
a chosen character but who's the narrator?
I guess it's just down to the puppet string maker.

The Book Of Armour

1989 was the year
she was bloated with glee
water retention, ocean eyes was her theme.
Fat thighs, swelled ankles, a fetus hides.

Behind two layers
skin and armour combined,
but little does a newly born mind
It just has hopes to survive
like every other human, the role of mankind.
So twelve months later
the summer of May shines
a mother cooked and mined all her life
her womb of metal serving a back handed surprise
her wolf told her now was the right time.
She can feel the baby kick and push
pining and whining her husband tells her to shush
she reclines and relies on what she confines
another love that keeps her happiness alive.
She's given up on the man she now has learnt to despise
a new-born baby keeps her hopes alive.

Her armour now stronger she holds it tight
her truth is where it lies
now a mother, a husband replaced
she or him can't differentiate,
nor can they see straight
now a big responsibility on their plate.

The Book Of Armour

Cannibalism is taboo
but what really is the difference
when you're waiting in queue
behind a man that makes your love wait in lieu,
back to the future,
back date to a fragile state,
truth is only realised when we are fashionably late.
Attachments are what we build to be immune
but Rome wasn't built in a day, it helps people get through.

A cycle to lose
a cycle they can't oppose
life moves so fast it's over before they'll know
4 little words, "I told you so."
So what's the point to make your move
when it's over before you can give what you owe
life doesn't tell us, our secrets show it
the answers were always there, we just chose to tow it.

Father still defiant
stronger than an ox,
little does his child know, he's caught the chicken pox
The Status Man's drive could never be manoeuvred, he could never be outfoxed,
a recipe of disaster for the lambs that don't fit in his box.

Working away like a slave
motivated by the shame
everything else is to blame
except for a status, his reputational gain.

As their child grew older
a mother and father, turned the thermostat to cool and colder.
Together by physics but homelessly extrinsic
mimicking unity his son didn't buy or believe it
all he could see was a father too busy, gaining likes from his community.
Mother too sad, too unhappy
her image of a perfect life started to look ever so ratty.
to her delight her yearly membership with Virgin renews
luckily for her, a corner shop approves.
American Express to her own expense
weaker by the day her mind is a mess,
her other half goes from strength to strength.
The Status Man tries to keep his ego intact
discrediting every other being.
Licking his fingers
newspaper flicking
eyes twitching,
his fingers pointing at the status quo
cursing celebrity entrepreneurs
his insecurity feeds the fear of his competitors
a man of champion drive but his heart of finishes well behind.
Dreary woes, religious men impose
sacrilegious opinions as he loathes.

Everything means nothing to him
but one thing signifies one meaning
a Status Man,
the only thing he believes in.

The Book Of Armour

He's married to a status
without the wedding ring
church bells rang
his child is now a man
a mother high but her health went down and down,
ten bottles later spirits drank and downed
a game of empty rummy bottles was this one child's playground.

He gambled every day in hope he banks
but disappointment concurred with each year that leapt
wasted treasured moments for a status that easily forgets.
A binman who dumped the ones who are silently dependent
a love debt on the account holders head but irresponsibility
he leaves the signal on red.
A family filled with wishful thoughts that their sadness will transmit
they pray each day that their father and husband's mind
will click and collect.

Immature minds
hearts of rock
for adolescents, an ability to be water frustrates and clots.
Every child's father is a hero
for every woman without a man is a widow,
once you see behind the mask
in a millisecond you'll be transported from fantasia to Earth.

*For a man who cannot live without an armour
is a man with a stump
helpless and reliant love victims have no choice but to swallow,
unconscious to the damage
the rooted sit around
a Status Man living in a paradise battlefront.
At war with his emotions "They're alright" says
his selfish delusional assumptions.*

*He only lives for a shot of an adrenaline buzz
and his home cooked dinner grub
6 a.m. up at the ready
stepping over his boy holding a teddy
he gets in from a day's work walks past his fragile brittle lady
10 p.m. a come down steady
12 a.m. sleeping, dreaming of money, money, money.*

*This is the daily life of The Status Man
a philosophy others wrote with his own right hand
it's black magic,
its sorcery a fucked up religion just to hold onto his integrity.
Nocturnal a family blinks he flies by
there is a kink,
a missing link,
a household with a jinx, voodoo, a sphinx.*

*Two bats turned upside down, burning in the light of a vampire's lunch
blood pouring from his canines it's all insanity
he needs therapy to help his psychology.*

*He strives each day to redeem and recover, his comfort milk and honey hunger
The pull of his thirst to protect his own interests
bloody trenches for a fighting knight,
dented and cut deep from his past
a pathway no one can get close enough to
for he is no empath
to what he endears to be true.*

*His status
his protection
his hope,
his preacher
his Rabbi
his Pope,
to him all was well
but for his loved ones a very slippery slope.
Dirty laundry
he dropped the soap
to protect the workings of his mind,
so in life…
A Status Man can cope.
Reputation and respect kept him feeling whole
but in order to give he knew he stole.*

The Book Of Armour

Things that didn't mean much were overdue to pay
his only son signed on the dole, his wife kept saying; "Are we ok?"
For her hubby, things took their toll which snowballed and rolled
so he built a barrier higher than the Berlin Wall,
a mother and wife sank... Sank deeper and deeper into a black hole.

Directionless input for his child
this home is no place for a young man to cope
for emotion was a thing for other people to sing
a vacuum cyclone designed for a win
life for his family was life on a wing.
A living death is the hardest thing
a jar emptying was a daily and occurring,
an emotional disconnection.

They both had to learn the hard way
a spouse so beat up and low
life for her was swept too far to row.
The black crow now rests upon his soul
a narrow vision, a head on collision
with wisdom that he just can't yet envision.
A sad state but a necessary trait
for life is ruthless it blew out her flame.

Passion is designed but for an intervention called fate
for some may even die due to the lack of compassion others cate
it's not for the hearts that feint
but the people that survive
armour is built to protect from the gas the hurt ones light.

The Book Of Armour

Two wrongs don't make a right
but to be alive is to fight
his father doesn't realise his own destructive device.

A healthy obsession but a Pandora box of confessions
with indiscretion he abandoned his spirit without concession,
sole focused on the respect he receives every time he's mentioned.
As time went quickly by, he missed the most special gift of two big brown eyes
for the presenters of presents hopes and innocence
the man with no presence was already unravelling white ribbons.
He was winning in their own demise,
he was dearly missed
for a wife and a kid that are left to drift.
Ocean waves picked apart and left to drown
he refused to take them to solid ground,
tied together by circumstance
legs hidden frantic paddling to the swan lake dance,
a family pleaded for a different stance,
a lifeboat?
A raft?
Support is what they desperately needed to craft
but for the unarmoured far too hard of a task.
Sharks surrounded a mother of one
life was ready to feast
happiness is a practice
and for a father to ease,
an enjoyable life for his family, their hope had decreased.

The Book Of Armour

For a Status Man's mind is impossible to keep sane
if not for a choice of character but to play his own game

his previous life an excuse his right to cause pain.
His past life was a significant excuse too much of a bane
he was levitating through life like David Blaine
he was oblivious for what he had become
this is called the trick of the trade.
He holds the key but for what is his purpose to be,
eyes in which he cannot see the wood before the trees.
An audience applause, which he redeemed
a one-dimensional shape a manmade disease
a not so helpful way, for one to falsely appease,
with what he tried to alt and delete.
He was determined to hide
a chosen character replaced what he lost inside.
In essence the truth was always there
he knew the secret an antidote to cure his care.
Ruthless measures had to be taken
for love was on the line
a mutation takes place
for every single face that needs saving
imperative to encase.
Our thoughts, guarded by the skull
it's called the evolution of the soul.

The Status Man looked up to Elon and Bill Gates
with a belief that heaven awaits.
A determination kept all he had
for he had too much at stake.
Self-made
status named
it could not be tamed
people's approval
the love he rates.

His job
his principle
a foundation he laid
his confidence built upon inflation, propaganda acquaints
only to hilt a weapon by his innate.

The hard comings of life he had been dealt, were defeated in the end.
With determination and obsession an armour was formed
his confidence alike started to soar.
A final admission that it helped his remission
the workload meant a laser vision
foresight unwrapped only focused on the present
nothing else was worth to mention
just a desire to move to crush prevention.

The Book Of Armour

A man of name
a status from shame
brittle inside
he learnt to play the game
a deal was made
in an uncompromising way
he had zero feelings
he felt no shame.

A love that turned to steel
he made a vow, his master restored
a key to unlock a padlocked door.

The Status Man traded hearts,
a business shmuck
a vessel of bucks
his morals and value sunk.
High risk bonds
he never shared
investing nothing
He did not care.
The greatest illusionist Houdini was in awe to stare.

Life to him was a game of rummy
with spiked shoes, he was running on an empty tummy.
For other people's opinions are his crumbs
this was enough
for a hungry Status Man who couldn't see through the rough.

The Book Of Armour

His shield reflected,
it deflected,
it reiterated that this was the only way
for a Status Man to stop becoming obliterated or insane.
A ticking time bomb
everything but himself he'd eliminated,
a lover of himself
a lover controlled by an endeavor of clout.

A servant to his own amendment,
not even the death of loved ones could fix this man's discontentment,
a bone headed man he hung, from torn tendons
a situation not desired by creators or decedents.

The problem just worsens
trapped encased with metal hearts
the fallen angels
hidden agendas from poisonous darts.
Living for independence
playing a mole
respect is given
appearance of a dutiful role.

His household now waterlogged in silent cries
6 a.m. sun light rise,
each piece of the family's jigsaw disappears
for each morning The Status Man doesn't say goodbye.

The Book Of Armour

Only his blood and his other half scream
living day by day in obscurity,
a titan at war but from outside it looks serene
for biological clocks it looks obscene
mesmerised and bewildered by insecure dreams.
Weeds grew bigger than his seeded ways
weeds diminished by hunger pains
people are victims of the hunger games.
Craved by the same people that hold the same name
strangers put on pedestals, life lessons made
rules designed and an armour to hide
that's what gives a Status Man time, a resting place to die.

Blood pouring from where she weeps
The Status Man doesn't hear, he walks when he sleeps.

Losses and winning chimes
time is non-existent, he doesn't comply
as long as he's admired by his peers, to him all is fine.
People give him the right to carry on
a vicious cycle
his loved ones hang on.

*A hope he will change but in order for things to be rearranged
The Status Man must fall on his sword by his own accord
a sacrifice is needed for a heart to be yours.
Thus we mourn as the rain doesn't stop to pour
the only chance of a miracle, is for him to be reborn.
As children need nothing but games of hide and seek
rehearsals for life with no choice, but to turn the other cheek.
A character chosen by all
a new development with no foresight
for a Status Man's offspring and wife.*

This is what they call: ***"The hardship of life."***

The Book Of Armour

THE MATERIAL MAN

*M*other's Day comes but for this child just another day
as the only bond he felt, was when he was cramped in a stomach of veins
May was his month, the day of 23.
Years had flown by
no wind beneath his wings, he still doesn't understand what the word love means,
every exam he failed dismally
a reflection of his parents, that cheated their matrimony.
Head teachers contacting with digits about a number
questioning his concentration level,
Elephant disease mentioning
therapy delegating
stripped naked in a room playing doctors and nurses
his birth markings concerning, nothing's working,
special need shirking
the only thing they could find was the pain beneath lurking.
Nightmares are shaken off in the presence of his mother,
how? Because they are the same as each other.
A mother drowning herself for she had no armour
she rejects life and all its trauma.
A child, now a young man learning the ropes of life,
things now seem clearer for the son of a broken wife.
His T-shirt marked in red dye
but still believes in blue when he looks to the sky,
feet on brown soil as he's judged and put on trial
a heap of emotion now in a pile
the young man building an armour out of iron.

Her child 9 going on 30
school in spring
you can smell the pine
a child starting to see the sign of the times.
A child starting to feel a certain quench for an answer
a child starting to see behind the armour
a child either cries or lives for humour
but the void inside grows like a tumour.
It tightens around his heart
his father's words, as trustworthy as a rumour
for his mother nothing soothes her.

Flesh and blood
Vodka shots, her booster
her glass picked up, she knocked it back
Brandy fires her coal, her Coke is flat
her child takes another jab.
For children not on the right path, everything is a stab in the dark.
A child still searching to find his X & Y's
without a map it takes forever
a lifetime to stretch out every strain
brought up by 2 people
strangers of the same name.
A child staring down the stairs
hearing arguments of their loving wares
he covers his ears and imagines he's in a cave,
he hoped… But failed to block out the sound waves.

The Book Of Armour

He turns the television up, but it just creates echoes of octaves
F minors
F sharps
F majors
F life, only the armoured are favoured
that's what couples call endearment,
but not for the vulnerable.
The white flag waivers
the down and out immersers
the systems best customers,
the tablets testers
the blind mice biopsies
supply the experimenters.

His mother's hand sliding across the bannister
he starts to pray hoping she makes it,
she walks up the stairway off balance with one glass of water
a risk taken from her husband's allowance.
Poisoned and intoxicated, she tries to make it to bed
fully clothed, she's comatose
dreaming of nothing, blank and indisposed.
A child in need sitting, wishing she could be freed from her vice that has his mother's
love, clamped and ceased.
His father didn't offer her a tonic
he's too busy maintaining the status quo,
but the child is resilient stoic and low.
Hurting but emotions can't be heard or shown, her love is not shared
nor is there a desire for preservation, just her despair.

Just another soul hanging in limbo
wishing on a star listening to Ringo,
now the 90's have come and gone
for her son's naivety was a handicap, a death card at birth
he was labelled a joker and a farce.
A question he just couldn't answer or get past
"For why am I so unhappy?" He sighed,
"Does happiness have to be rebirthed?"
"Can happiness be something that stands alone itself?"
It's called the everlasting effects of a dysfunctional coincidence.

"Detention!" *His teacher said.*
The young boy calls his mum for reassurance
as the school made a wrong conclusion
a phone call to his mother, bewildered and scared
but Mum's too drunk to focus or care.
So, he sat staring at the white wall
he laughs inside no trigger was pressed
to him this is his default, a normal feeling of suppress.
A young man with very little in the tank
a mother screaming, "Why are you wasting the black?
You are not going to get a job, you're pulling a prank."
For now, a young man's armour was shattered
defenceless from her attack
he tried his hardest to battle through, it was the only thing he could do.
Now he's gotten a little older
once a dreamer now a realist an acceptance of what his household is.
Watching as a spectator, an umpire, a commentator
he needs to play by his own rules
a disruptive routine for a child inside that's still teething.

The Book Of Armour

He lives alone in his room as life's too gloomy
a young man starving
laying in bed for 3 days, his mother is drunk
he can't handle her ranting displays
he weren't strong enough.
The Status Man still astray
sometimes he had crazy thoughts like smashing his mother over the head
with her own ashtray.
To his son's dismay, he could hear his father laughing
while his wife sits next to him in pain,
a role he simply chose and betrayed.
Parents sitting directly under wooden floors
where M&M wrappers, and crumpets are stored,
he curls up in a ball
eyes closed and so was his door.
His bedtime was set at dawn
his day was black with no stars to follow or align
he dreads to get out of bed to face the swine
while his father fails to act, to a Status Man everything is fine.
A young boy conditioned to believe; this is normal, presumably.
a broken person's perception is a pantomime, masks and costumes
a lesson never learnt we only assume
the sane are turned, the insanity will resume.

This is the illusion, an example made of a Material Man
a character formed from the love of what he earnt
expensive materials were his only concern,
an armour forced on,
so he could forget what he had experienced before.

The Book Of Armour

It only took 20 years for a Material Man to be born
a man in his own right,
his parents and him never saw eye to eye.

Now more knowledgeable
the situation more tolerable,
wiser than his years but still abused and bullied by The Status Man's old dear.
His confidence was lost in the abyss
nobody to witness or address to shift.
A situation that is a bloody mess
a child born from his mum and dad's kiss
a pulse given without a promise to exist.
An exile of honesty his life a tragedy,
a bully protected
a father in denial.
He only lived for the rhapsody of praise
he'd let his wife do what she's done for a decade.
His son turning crazy from all the degrade
scars not healed from the scabs that grazed.
The man of the house
hard externally but cowardly unaware
a mentally ill family affair,
totally broken impossible to repair.

The child's prayers finally ran out
God could only do so much,
his mother fell down the stairs of heaven
a dent in the wall in her partner's act of oppression.

The Book Of Armour

Unarmed and fragile, she tumbled to a heap
unconsciously she lived in forever deep sleep,
empty, undernourished she was close to death.
The Status Man stood in a corner as quiet as a mouse
no responsibility for his pretend love,
his spouse now a product of what she went without.

The son angry, bitter and in disgust
he fell to depression and complete despair
he knew he had to choose a character to wrestle or to bare
he feared following the truth
due to his misguided youth,
he really wasn't prepared just like his mother; he couldn't climb the stairs.
Life to him just didn't seem fair
a pat on the back and well-dones were rare.
He needed a confidence boost as joy was aloof
so, he learnt the hard way
from a boy to a man, he proudly stood
so he decided to press the button to reboot.
He closed his eyes and chose to dare
he said, "It's time to live a lie, I vowel to never cry again!"

A new player emerged in this evil game
he wanted to become a millionaire
to wash his dreary past ways.
And with that,
a character was chosen
a ringleader for criterial
on the basis of consumption and material.

The Book Of Armour

He cried one last time and closed his eyes
he chose to dare to play the game
to devote his time to materialism and made an oath to never share,
he knew he needed to shape his emotions and to separate them in pairs,
lost but now found, he was once outside defeated and tried.
Investments in jewels and stocks
now just another man in the lost property box.

Conditioning himself, he said he forgot
questions from the past
he refused to ask
he finally had a purpose, a goal
something that helped him cope.
The more he purchased the longer his rope
the longer the rope the more he didn't mope
the less he moped the stronger his grope,
the stronger the grope the more unarmoured people choked.

Finally, a breakthrough life was controlled
life was his and now finally owned.
He outcasted anyone that didn't fit his image and click
he didn't know what friendship was
his accountant and bank manager spoke to him as the boss.
NFT's and Crypto currency's
he pocketed change that his mother passed into his hands
a belief that he had more than he had
the days of his old man's status, were thrown in the dam
memories and money washed down with Baby Sham.

The Book Of Armour

*High class escorts every other night
drugs and nightclubs and condo skylights,
Versace bath robes
Coco Chanel soaps,
with 1st class flights and brown envelopes.
He lived in the noughties
Miami vice a reality,
for each endorphin rush
six bedrooms in Beverly Hills was bought then sold
with each time his self-esteem felt low.*

*A balancing act
lying on his loral just wasn't enough
armour attached but feelings couldn't match
he just wouldn't let himself get side-tracked.
A material seclusion brainwashed by designers
Valentino, Diane, Manolo
boujee discos, midnight living with mottos of YOLO.
Belly and head bloated by assets, vultures quoted
Philosophical iconicity as security rose
a man so high on life
a drone for a human, built from a pitch perfect pound note.
Buzzing infected hums bursting from his own interpretations
a man that doesn't question, why's, where's and what's.
Ignorant to the sound of rhythm and blues
he only rides waves from Bang & Olufsen's,
fabricated objects were the only things he would allow to stay
over the years he was built to damn,
the rain tried to erode the pain,
but no resistance could ever break the silence of the lamb.*

*Badges and brands but not wise enough to understand
the destination is where the mind lands.
Sound proofed from defenseless authenticates
dangerously close of a replication
the surrogate of an experiment was his vindication
a man-made potion it's called the antidote for cerebration.
He doesn't see a pattern
he's in full stride
his eyes tinted by red roses
violets of blues died.*

*A family tree constricted with tears of Vodka liquid
his family all afflicted,
The young man had to learn quickly
to survive… You must be addicted.*

*The Material Man had a beautiful life
a routine of driving through Mayfair, he parked outside
using his private parking space
his gloves prevent touching a past he erased.
He doesn't want to be contaminated by anything that his mind will let last
his favourite café called the Concerto
classical music and chandeliers
The Material Man at the pinnacle of all his banished fears.
Thanks to a shafter, a master plan
a reaching of his crescendo,
an ambient reflection marked with depth, of visual marbled imperfection.*

Outside it's cold but inside homely and full of mold
skeletons in closets that a war couldn't solve
fabrics disguised the rolls,
an exterior that locked the vault
a surrounding oversized with luxury of entitlement, he gloats with pride.

Proud and defiant he sat in a corner
reading the Financial Times
hiding behind Victorian plating, done up to the nines.
Time to him was fabrication, a precarious ghostly cry
it was impossible for The Material Man's mind to quantify,
for it was too hard for this well-off man to summarise.
Impossible for The Material Man's mind to quantify
a love for shiny things DNA of a magpie,
99.9
0.01 dogmatic, invisible and dumb.

His gold reading glasses appeared above the New York Times,
his fate was written.
A lady dressed in her own disguise
a beautiful new asset an incredible light, beamed into his eyes.
A lady in black trousers and a buttoned-up shirt
she was a combination of sexy and smart
he ordered a cappuccino with cream on top
she said, "Certainly sir, do you take sugar with that?"
He said, "I used to, but now my life is sweet to the max." She smiled,
then turned her back, he was staring behind Gucci shade of black.
She was pinning her hopes as he was holding back
the naughty things he craves, she was already picturing her engagement ring
both were royal built on wobbled founding's.

Two people as the Twin Towers
king and queens in their own rights
their lives were copied and pasted
same story but on a different page.
She walked over dropped the receipt
a service charge she added on
pound note signs on a blank page,
a new chapter for her to finally escape her maze.
They both found a value and chose the price
enlightenment they had found but a false perception,
a shadow that followed them around
nobody holds a life manual or a Bible when down,
it's universal
a pandemic of Gemini foes,
no symmetry or Co.
A generational cycle of division in the fabric people have sewn
the cause is of phycological trauma with an inner request to postpone,
two pupils self-taught that didn't want to listen
for what their destination had brought.
Switched off walking in the air
daydreaming with no care
now it's too late, the natural purity of themselves shall never reappear,
a pair that will never suit
but at least the monsters stayed locked away.

The Material Man's paid his way for peace to obey
so did she, but only for a cosmetic change.
He vowed to fund her aesthetics and tighten what's loose
The Material Man pulled proudly a Parker from his suit.

*He manufactured a prosthetic donation to lend
words written from a pen told her a promise to leave, he faithfully kept.*

*So, she quit the very next morning at 10 a.m.
she spent the afternoon tarting herself up
he beeped right outside her eyes wide, her mouth dropped.*

*As she stepped in his hot shot ride
chat wasn't flowing but endorphins were in with the tide
both not knowing
the essential mechanical ongoings
Two brains ill and sick, internally still loading.
Both still seeking a lift
hidden motives
storages full and impossible to erase,
space is added by plastic cards of trade.
Servants cleared and indebted by degrade
half human, half-made
evolution of a person impossible to evade.
Colours of greys and golds, there's no getting away from a bad phase
it cuts deeper than the Mariana Trench
it imprints you, from your very first day.*

*Identities riddled with insecure dreams, incurable cancerous white and black cells
an aspiration to pick up themselves, where people get hurt and fall down.
Dementia is an antidote to a life of rage
memories are desired by misguided players that play the game.*

Material Man.
Aesthetic Girl.
From the outside their life looks like couple goals,
but from the inside
a fridge ominously cool,
heated money
burning genitals.
Their situation got more difficult than Einstein, Hawkins, Carl Friedrich Gauss
algebra, geometry and calculus.
A mind scrabbled by a yearning of Caziques.
An agreement to swap
one gives head the other gets neckless
a nightmare to God's sight
a dream for the majority crying at night
debilitating and incurable for innocent lives.

Fast forwarding a quarter of her life
she's tried to take all he's got
just because she knows, she's hot.

He's fucking her in every hole
both stealing from each other what their yesterday stole
two years now gone, germs transferred
tonsil tennis, ping pong, Tetras,
Instagram comments of fire are burnt.
Gas on the stove, cooked romantic and cursed
LOL's shared by bots behind their backs
what they desperately wanted, they finally achieved.

The honeymoon was a farce but a duty to proceed with a ring of bouquets
Champagne flowing in the month of May
bells rang
spectator's tongues out,
perception of invincibility was never in doubt.
An armoured forcefield to their troubles
it began and amounted from a toddler who'd tantrum and shout.
How the truth lies in the early years
when money and mirrors couldn't dry their tears,
the more complex they became
the more they didn't take account of how their innocence wasn't to blame,
the more they'd adorn the more things they would count on.
All she's left with is a selfie to pout, that hid her inner woes
to let her relive the innocence that is now decomposed.
once a girl now a woman just clinging on
dreams and thoughts of being loved and adored
for this Aesthetic Girl on the inside is lost in defraud.
She was left with no choice
the pain was too much
it was her only and last resort,
her exterior now built
a hardened shell
unrecognisable,
in the eyes of others, she excelled.

she painted a perfect picture
a graphic life
magazines of Elle and Vogue,
she had finally achieved how she wanted it to be
a concept modelled and materialised by an armoured mannequin
for The Material Man was happy with how things panned out,
his world dripping with orgasm a climaxing hydration to his drought.
He chased 6 seconds of pleasure, a pound coin
each time the moments phased out
a partnership business deal,
each player in their element of thrill.

With steely eyes, she defiantly lied
to stop her feelings melting
a maiden of ice.
There was no time to hide or flutter
but unfortunately for The Aesthetic Girl,
The Material Mans bread was buttered,
without a care he's head was turned by a young stripper
she laid it all bare,
undeniably disloyal
sentimentally empathetical
cruel and unethical
created by an imbalance of the chemicals.
7 days a weakness to all
sins absorbed a character to act a fool,
her shining armour had been foiled
a bolt cutter with pliers of iron.

For one moment her front was displaced
she was moved inside by dismay
it took her by surprise she felt emotion behind her eyes, in such a very long time.
She needed someone to remind her it was alright to cry
her broken wings were clipped by the ugliest thing
the rug pulled beneath her pedicured feet
her fur coat murdered and lynched
just a nameless female abandoned by Louis V.

The red underfloor of her 6 inches,
hammered to the pavement rooted by skin
a fallen angel now set free, an exorcism by the most natural of things.

Synthetic and leathered she found herself, she removed the cover
all thanks to her very sick mother.
She relied on her husband
his money was promised
but white lies proved to be right
it was paper-thin, a dishonest sovereign.
Her mother kept alive by her daughters hustling
her exploits weren't enough
an act of love
blindly miscued and managed to change her mother's cancerous blood.

The Book Of Armour

An incurable disease
two people dying by the same thing,
hidden with a mask that can't be seen.
The Material Man caused despair to everyone's lives
to whoever he crossed paths with and whoever arrived
to him everything is a play toy,
black magic and voodoo dolls, one minute he loves you the next your banal.
His feelings were lost, a long, long time ago
life lessons that his parents chose not to nurture and grow
his armour now too strong and to fitted to go.
Destruction by nerves of steel
his heart has now stopped by the pace of the wheel.

A blood clot from the high barred bars of his cot
now deadlocked, he only lives for the adrenaline shot.
He uses the same key for everything
always on the lookout for the next beauty spot,
a selfish tornado
a force so unstoppable
nobody to deplore his actions raucous and unpredictable.

The Material Man's running riot
substituting his vowels
by taking advantage of what God allowed.
Earth plates shift as a reminder he stands in-between
cursed and blessed by an adolescent state
he never seemed to grasp or redeem.

A teenager lost forever
a newfound love for happiness flings
a divorce now on the cards
solicitor and court hearings with love and protection barred.
It's now a hazard
Two pieces of a metal shard
a girl aesthetically cute
a contest between beauty and the truth she mutes.
The Material Man's admiration computes
he decided it was time to move on to something shiny and new.
So, she went back to square one,
a waitress trying to allure with the next web she spun
her efforts begun to trap another mother's son
a nightmare catcher she flung,
knowing he will get it all back to front.

As for The Material Man, he didn't care
he got on with his affair
one man's trash is another man's treasure,
he could only self-love.

After only one month
her name he couldn't remember
he parked in his private space outside the Mayfair Café.
He walked through the door like nothing ever happened
sat down in the same armchair and proceeded to read the demographic column
a waitress of no thought, labelled as Old Mother Hubbard.

A waitress walked over and bowed down to honour his rich persona
he smiled and without hesitation reordered,
a booby trap, a queen of her quarter,
while he felt like a king sipping on rose water.

Bitter and sour, a malted daughter
he picked up another guardian's waste
littered her with all what he bought her.

He continued in the same vein
two people in desperate need of a life support machine.

A wife's crown was found in the court
new recruits that were never built to last
enjoying the labors of their fruit
both astute and both built to pursue,
a past they desperately tried to refute.

The Book Of Armour

Dilution of a soul but a caricature
a cycle that brought them both back to the start,
two children hiding from a root to branch.
They didn't know where their greatest strength lied
an armour they hid and coward behind
an exterior armour so powerful that lied,
to themselves and others combined.

The Book Of Armour

THE AESTHETIC GIRL

Orphaned and not wanted
no home of her own
for it was always a full house,
different door knockers and different bell rings,
every time it was a no, her tears would sting.
An angel that needs a guardian
she just wanted something to cling on to,
children are strong
born in murky waters
every day a lonely daughter's life alters,
her confidence slaughtered
her only routine is speaking to the next lawyer.
Autumns pass and still no offers
bunk beds and firm mattresses
she doesn't see living as a necessity.
She doesn't know if she is coming or going
running or slowing
she's a mixture of them all,
her emotions flowing.
She tried desperately to reminisce
about a mother's kiss,
her ignorance is her naivety,
she's always busy dreaming.

She blows hot and cold
sour lemons or pepper mint
tongue biting then wincing, skin pinching
but knows no different,
for she shares a bunk bed and eats food from the canteen kitchen.
Communal one for all,
sharing
laundering
always moving.
A princess in a dungeon
she calls it her home
locked away due to circumstance.
Every time she enters a family a bow,
she's shown the door and told she needs to find a new place to go.
She dreams of being wanted
she's fed up with being picked up then halted,
Scavenging in the dustbins but defiant she won't succumb
she refuses to throw in the stained white towel,
a woman's strength is her greatest device
an under belly so soft
as she plays and acts in a cast of ice.
A performer with her strings pulled
eyes feared
her future is her present
replayed past weirs.
She questions if her expectations are wrong and obscene
nevertheless, once or twice she OD'd.
She got out fixed up her act and took the lead
used her animal instinct,
a cockroach looking for a sugar cube, ready to feed.

The Book Of Armour

A belief, a girl's aesthetic is all she needs
it's the only thing she fully trusts
it's all cosmetically made up.
Sexually falling ass-over-tit,
corsets and chicken fillets, enhance the imagery.

Explicit visionary of a businesswoman
a loophole monetised for adultery,
if only she realised the after taste causes a knock-on effect,
O' the hunger, O' the savagery.

So, she created a way that made her feel wanted
lipstick and eye shadow, she flaunted.
Breasts pushed up and low-cut vests
an explicit sexual reality for men to caress.
Spending nights in many men's beds,
feeling wholesome this was her defense.
She learnt to invest in her own masterpiece
the lower her dignity, the less side-effects to appease,
the armour she chose, was a life of aesthetics.
She worked as a waitress on the side
to earn ends meet to support her grind.
She loved the compliments with precious words from strangers that defined,
from the outside she looked fine
but inside she felt ugly,
like a drug user she needed her fix
she hid behind the character of an imperial minx.

Concealer, her Polyfilla
a desire for wealthy men
her soul as cold as Russia
her quest for love
a confession kept close,
in which she suffers.
A body shaped like a Coke bottle
a self-taught professional
she had her life mapped out,
a lifelong treasure hunt
her compass, her cunt.

Platinum and golds
pearls, diamonds and sapphires
all it took was a ruby plumped pout
her ammunition for now
her weapon of choice
but gone in a flash,
she wasn't to know
even steel rusts
covered like a contagious rash.

She didn't know any different
she wasn't spoilt to find out
a dirty correlation to Roxanne living with red lights and sass.
Dribbling mouths eager to pounce
crowds selling only to trounce
self-worth she couldn't pronounce,
short-changing herself
pleasurable sounds, exchanging to pounds.

Five men a night
amounted to a plastic life
how many? She didn't stop to count.
She only cares about the present
a slave to sterling and her German bank
a calculation, she couldn't work out.
An orderly sadistic route
a wish for protection
a hope of a wealthy addition
due to a practiced tried and tested rendition,
A stitched incision
she's on a mission
running on an admission of guilt.

Piled on pressure and late nights
he spilt her milk,
her crying eyes have turned upside down
her life now tilting
a delusional happy world view.

She planned her life to a T
except for the morning after toilet coughs and wet dreams
working in a café in Mayfair to achieve her dream,
she knew she had to manifest to gain a happy mean.
Her past she needed to digest
she was a spy behind Victorian forks and knives
a loving spoon couldn't be picked up, it was out of sight.

Eagled eye
all her dignity pushed aside
a vulture an opportunist
a determination to find,
a someone to fulfil her satisfaction and be wined and dined.

A man walks in holding the Financial Times
his eyes hidden,
her pupils multiplied in size.
Minimising the chances of a plan being figured out
two desperate people
two professionals
one prerogative
made and given,
helped by a master card
blood pressure was risen.

She knew this was the guy to fill the void of pain,
right before her very eyes
under her breath adamantly said, "That's mine"
she used her hips to turn around
she applied her lipstick
scurried over a self-declared servant
for a man who was willing to oblige,
and give her a life of sweets sherbets and Turkish delights.
Disguised as a waitress, a pleasant curse and surprise
for a Material Man's life, a conceptual diagram
to worship the next object
his displeasure a guide.

The Book Of Armour

They mimicked and mimed
captivated eyes caught up by their narcissistic lies
an aim to take what each other can provide
selective to protect an arsenal they both faced,
a bunker to hide.

He gave his best chat up line
calling her sweet and a sight for sore eyes
so, she hopped, skipped, and jumped to the coffee machine,
she pretended to care about her 9-5 grind
she bided her time
she knew she was about to hit her prime.

Her life was methodically designed
every step she climbed
to the top she snapped, crackled and popped,
she never gave in
she refused to stop
her past was pushing her to achieve her wildest dreams;
Julia Roberts, Angelina Jolie
she lived in a fantasy of pretty woman movies scenes.
Designer shops and Lamborghinis
a cosmetic Barbie girl she wished to be
holidays in Switzerland to ski.
Luxurious bags colours in all three,
along with sparkly diamanté.
She was always at the hippest places to be
V.I.P memberships at chic award ceremonies
her expectations had superseded,
a new life for a victim of a past that always impeded.

Immoral and corrupt
a capitalist life
no cost or expense to low or high,
her pain is numbed
smashed blown to smithereens
she walks over with a coffee cup in hand
this woman's use is to carry a brand.
Her eyes analysing all that sheens
her head in the clouds
a twinkle in the eyes
aiming for the stars, waves of emotion
dictated by what shines in the dark.

He stands proud and grand
a man in demand
total control
a power to behold.
She gambles
and plays Russian roulette
based on trust,
her hidden issues are polished
her nails sit heavy on the trigger
her itchy palms await after her audition.

The Material Man pulls out a parker pen
she's looking down the barrel
she started to think is it hell or heaven?
He writes her requisition
his handwriting was exquisite
eleven number digits.

The Book Of Armour

A life of retirement for an exchange
metaphoric and literally
a deal conspired by a Material Man that admired her physically.
A high valued man inspired
a life of perfection and beauty
she had finally peaked
The Aesthetic Girl had finally achieved.
Years from her teens with hopes and dreams
of becoming the next big thing,
a concept built upon Kimmy K, Kylie J with an attitude of Beyoncé.
A warped ideology
a belief it's her only opportunity,
the past tense of troubled obscurity now on the brink of jubilee celebratory.

She swallows her guilt with the prescription of a happy pill
she's a patient in intensive despair
all she needs is some unconditional care,
floating with gravitational flair
She accepts, a proposal from a man whose just as scared.

A napkin stained insured her with a derisive future to bask
her mask was finally useful to complete her most important task.
A mission she was sent on
skills learnt from television
a trap door spider, spying on her next victim.
Glamourous scenes are now her reality
a man sucked in by her femininity.
Just another man caught up in her fishnet tights
the tightest man now as generous as Jesus Christ.

A worthwhile addition he blows like the wind
but a lady wearing what's in range and as the season begins
a materialistic man an owner bronzed by tan.
He stands up, walks out as it starts to rain
umbrellaed by names
two people burnt and frayed
but masterpieces framed by their own mindful ways.
Insane and scathed, deeply ashamed of their life before
bent and corrupt
they were not thinking from the heart.
A man with no balls
castrated by birth
her wound surfed
it picked her up from the turf,
wounded from an adverse life
she never tried, tried to unearth.
She turned to what she saw and heard
survival came in the form of a bird
wolf whistles were her calling card
it was the only way to soar and be of high regard.
Too many years clipped
too many years adlibbed
too many years slipped through her mits,
she was finally granted by he who permits.

The Material Man slipped on the slit of her skirt
advertised, succumbed in which he bought,
a deal, a bundle
a hand shaken with spit
a toot of his horn
24 hours had gone
she came running from her bedsit home.
He didn't care or correlate the link
into what is at stake
for the one who carries bearing fruit
he didn't see the clues,
she was mirroring the reflection of a material duce.
Far too busy licking his lips
excited to play with his shiny new toy in parts and in bits
a juicy apple glistening,
infront everything seemed greener
a bed for a petal the poisons in the nectar.

Begging to be munched
with thongs and thoughts of laurels
high scores of quarrels.
A meaningless life
a syringe of dopamine
she takes him orally,
underwear piling up
dignity on the marble floor,
the lowest low but a girl worshipping the head of a cock.
She was bred in distortion
it was never her fault
it's a cycle passed on, impossible to overwrite or uninstall.

The Book Of Armour

Two people trying to claw their way out of hell
both combusting from the inside-out,
where did it all go so wrong.

Extroverted tricks of the trade
an unethical tirade
but self-made by selfish desires of gain.

Her plan came true
she jetted down from a plane every step was now her runway,
a tissue for the blues.
Her wishes were granted
her endurance prevailed
her sadness tapered
a liaison hoaxed then put in separate boxes.
She relocated from the bottom to middle class
her happiness started to grow ever so fast,
Her smile beamed and every day she laughed
black and white pictures, saturated and sharp.

Her present to past
a total contrast,
a substance, or a farce
here today but will it ever last?

Humanity barred, now a compromise that's covered in scars
you must hunt then shaft, a shot thrown in the dark,
a dagger from a serial killer,
a blunt edge but to others a dart,
a throw that's gone too far.

The Book Of Armour

Oblivious to the murdering spree
defending herself, religiously
protected by expensive taste,
harmless but harmful covered in lace.

Heedless and armoured
an aesthetic bombardment
a material man who garnered
a temporary father
both desperate to hit their marker,
so, they both can materialise a stronger armour.
Golden showers
nose in powders
helicopters propelling into twin towers.
An orderly fashion crumbing from the seams
pinned together misleadingly
all for pretense, she sold herself short
she pretended there's a method to her madness a bae covered in salt.
Senses miscued,
enticed by the smell of a shop doorways perfume.
They lived like lovers but also lived with hate,
catered romantic dates
silver tray platter they lived like king and queen,
the reasons didn't matter.

The Book Of Armour

The heart cannot be renewed
pumped with adrenalin but still broken in tatters,
someone needs to pay for this mess
they rode off into the sunset
living in the moment
their skeletons were well kept.
Kept on a leash like a household pet
they kept each other's monster locked beneath and behind the iron fisted vents.
It was safe keeps
they stayed quiet to allow their innocence of a baby to sleep.

She kept daydreaming through life,
she's hot as hell but cold as ice
a vice, calculated and precise
resized and manufactured to entice
boxes and bags, a decorative excite.

The bright city lights
driving through Monaco
life's formula to spice,
peppered and chi
his and her grainy white lines,
two individuals in need of an exorcize.

Novelty living, for now
driven by betrayal and self-doubt
costing generations, chasing clout
market stools and betting touts
gamblers with meek and mild shouts,
wins turn to losses but they give it the benefit of the doubt.

Dog eat dog, corned and conned
people mourn and others sob
slaved to a job to feed 1% that are wired wrong,
but little did the newlyweds take the time to think
far too busy basking in the life they enrich.
Wagging and chasing their tails
to reach a ceiling and the holy grail,
holidays to Venice, Las Vegas
winter cabin cottages in Wales.

Exclusive packages at the Seychelles
Iceland trips on Benetti yachts
a year now passed
she's high flying in a fairy-tale,
a repetitive cycle
a chariot ride
merry go rounding the protected divine,
its pivotal to strive of that of Calvin Klein.
A cord that works to pull
the sound of a horn, loud sounds call
for an addiction to hoard
idolised IG girls abroad leads to invertebrates,
not broad enough to carry a spine.
A peaceful moment then suddenly her iPhone rang…
"Ring-Ring!", "Ring-Ring!"
It was hard for her to answer,
she had her hands full, she was applying her tan
she managed to answer with one eye that overpeered a 10-acre land.

The Book Of Armour

"Hello", a voice she sensed was one of her own
her mother suddenly got in distance to touch
she managed to deviate the subject over lunch,
The Aesthetic Girl was in shock,
the breaking news was all too much.
Her biological mother spilled the beans
she apologised with every breath she took
she broke the news of the life choices she chose,
a daughter in shock an imperium stone diminished the further it dropped.
Her onyx of healing was a misfortunate loan
bespoke thoughts, a concealer she believed she owned
overthrown by the power of just one phone call.
A mascara made up to shield from people throwing rocks
but diamonds don't last forever the black market conned.
But on the other hand, regrets of greener pastures stain your bones
in her eyes there was only one true love,
but now she must cooperate, she made a hard decision to help.
For she didn't want regrets at a later date
so she took more money than ever before
A con artist who died, now her mum's life support.
She was born in a show room,
a live auction for people to bid
a product of her environment,
a commodity for the richest robin in the hood.

Her mother's ill health was kept at bay
by her daughter's skill and self-sabotaging ways,
nurtured through her orphaned days
her life was now perfect and free to liaise.

The Book Of Armour

A deal behind her husband's back
due to a violent cancerous attack
her mother's dependent and hard cash strapped,
the pain intolerable,
a mother being mothered by an adolescent, who's just as fallible.
A husband naive but subliminally agrees
on provisos that she would still be a toy, that's his.
Things were working in threes all with different deceiving motivating means
money swapping hands to keep The Aesthetic Girl's mother alive
while her husband reliant on her to add to a materialistic way of life.

It keeps a trio going
it's their will to survive
A wife obsessed with mirrors, a perceptive surmise,
a reason to bury the memories for a loving family she pined.
She had no choice
she gave up and resigned
she was lost looking for a different sign.
She was a shepherd to the star, the only shining light
she believed it was only a matter, a matter of time.
She never questioned if it was a disservice to herself
to commit to the biggest crime, sex her only success from lonely rich guys.
She ran straight into the arms of the first man that asked
she felt a sense of value but really, she was a joke to somebody's last laugh.
she kept going in with desperation, she's never known anything to last,
her mother exiled but now reliant on her daughter's grasp,
they both knew it was there last and only chance.

Desperate needs, a measuring jar
ruled in favour when things get hard.

The Book Of Armour

You never really know what you might need until its gone
sorrow and euphoria counter, what's short and long
stereo types and radio songs
waves of magnitude
bygone will be bygones.

Naivety can kill
the world spins for thrills with no form,
happiness is born from sad spaces of noir.
Being rich or poor sits and rests on your natural perspective,
people are the cowards and warriors of war.
A hunger to roar
fire burning from the core,
not enough to go around
so, she generates more to ensure
her egos a God, worshipped and ridiculed.
Conscious people try to undo
the ignorance the greed of hisses and boos
a vigilante, an unlawful act to rectify the economy booms.

Outlaws of the jungle
concrete and smoothly serene
a drill to people's ears
drumming with fear
money doesn't sell what can cure and heal
treatment is given you can't sit nor kneel,
the final and only offer is to stand and be still.

The Book Of Armour

For this pretty Polly still had the world at her feet
with the added pressure, things looked bleak
but for the aesthetic girl there was no worry
for this girl has fleeted feet.
Her demands had risen
funds were dripped fed and given,
crumbs coated in treacle
unaware her master craved a new sequel,
nightmares she had but when she woke her coma continued.
Queen of his lair
queen of his stare
queen of a heart she wouldn't dare to lay bare.
The transactions he dealt and deemed to be fair
every day she fought to keep what she had intact,
but slowly she noticed a drought
she felt elbowed, cornered and flat.
Pussy fizzing
combed and pampered
brushed just like a domesticated cat
then tabbed as a fad,
tagged as easy and glad.
What's the big problem?
Lads will be lads
an open invitation to the highest bidder
as one girl's sad, another girl walks the plank.

Dead end alleys, no short-cuts just see-through pants
dangerous valleys, night foxes labelled as slags,
dirty dogs that cross off, in five tally shags.

They live in exchange of digits that transcend
faking it to make it, is their only way.
For an Aesthetic Girl, a heart that's desperate to defend
little she does to reamend.
Her liberty from pain
her honesty betrayed
she continues to reoffend,
she had realised that life is something you cannot pretend.
Rainbows of beauty are formed in the eye
a natural storm, The Material Man started to get bored
as so his interest started to fold,
the rose lens on his Ray Bans became disposable
her sun rays became cloudy and cold.
Branded bags from his wife's arm now gone
stripped from her accessories,
she started to merge into her Yves Saint Laurens
She was as replaceable as the items in her walk-in wardrobes.
Her glittery eyes were pawned
she was brought back to the reality of a dismal life, she tried to defraud and rectify.
The threshold of having his wife around became painful and thin
his serotonin ran out,
she resembled to him something rotten not ripe.
A distorted energy, an annoying gripe
The start of his story had crept back in,
the sadness referred and indexed to the end,
a first page he thought was contently in the bin.

*So, he made his way to his local strip club
women danced and polled
money flying from the pink light bulbs,
Queen heads dancing to Drake and Cardi B
men chanting, "Take it off! take it off!"*

*Frothing from the gums
ladies dazed and coked,
for 100 bills, they would gag and choke.
Motives of Fendi and Cadillac's
a risk of anthrax, one of many girls risking it all
acidic germs from old arthritic men
a woman's body is a deposit, again and again.
Inner littler girls did anything to escape
every girl a gambler, they have it all to do
a philosophy of all or nothing
 a job that needs thickened skin
and shoulders of chips
hearts penetrated by black jack's kiss.*

*Left to lady luck
masked and caped
living by a mathematical fate.
Its incurable,
an ex-lover of life living in a post-traumatic crunch
an effort to fight the black hole,
the void that mutates by the redundancy of her cunt.
Now feeding on her feelings of a past time euphoric mode
pure and cleansed obliviously on the mend
what she thought was good for her changed her psychological habits of spend.*

She was unbolted and deconstructed, a humanoid
it's all robotic and absurd
a behavior learnt to avoid.
A waste of oxygen
a generation in need of a detoxication, but the pain still bleeds
it shows every day in a man's ball cock and load.

As Bloody Mary blows
later Mary's hopes are sewn
pains of a period she can no longer solve,
a young girl influenced and dosed.
Young women chasing bread loaves
left in the toaster, melted plastic on burnt toast,
young daughters once, a father they roast
pillages, pilgrims, dim-witted supplied and fitted
with weapons of mass destruction born from King David.
Godlike horny and kitted,
tools as gifted as a mother's milky bitty titty.

One shot taken, a bullet for safety
she's open 24/7
available daily rate hours, sunrise and sunsets
God is praying begging for her sake,
egged on to take a vocational break
God as her witness,
a hope she would notice
man-made and fabricated, a baby oiled servant.
she doesn't stop, her status inflates,
her leg breaks every time she's on a podium or stage,
competitive strippers obsessed with an impossible task of what they can attain.

The Book Of Armour

A page from the oldest profession
no dignity or leaf, they'll continue to streak
a library they whisper their body crawls and creaks.

Clothes pinging off
men hypnotized their cocks harden
instinctual and desensitised, criminalistic acts upon each woman's rocking pride
closeted cries fall blind to an introduction of high fives.
The drug of ass smacks, a fix for selfish mankind,
out-of-sight-out-of-mind,
mentality is the word that the first three letters say they tried.

too much attention paid to a woman's outside
no empathy as they beat her insides to a silent cry.
Just another Aesthetic Girl whose skin sheds
then it thickens in a blink
it holds weight on every date
as she gambles, her coffin awaits.
Brain cells distracted in psychosis
a dirty mattress but sheets gold in satin
The Material Man whisks her away
a vacation for ten days,
while the wife sits at home and obeys.
Her layoff is paid
a rusty old toy has been sold to trade
then put back on display
her sunny blue skies are now clouds of shade.

The Book Of Armour

A silver lining, she prays she would once again be dame
she didn't give up what she felt the right to acclaim,
back to golden mining
as it's all been taken away.

Mother and daughter realigning but painfully dying
their straight road passages, now a roundabout spinning and spiraling.
Promises she made to her mother
promises that could not now be fulfilled,
they both relied on another person
happiness even further afield,
tired and barely fighting
they united in desperation to iron creases on the wall of writing.
Fishes now caught, reeling with guilt
conscience barbecued, grilling burnt and cooked.
The Material Man's paid for a new upgraded toy,
no one can rain on a one-man band he openly plays his life,
a game in hand.
He marinades his new chick in promise of a romantic serenade
a swab and a swap, his ass is licked
a new girls happiness is saved with one finger bent and flicked.
His ex-wife a cascade
sadness once again, was blown like a grenade.
A ticking time bomb for the victims of a previous hard life,
reliant on luck, a bingo game
for one girl out of the cave
another girl's aesthetic, deteriorates and fades.
Each girlfriend's chance of a rebuild dramatically drops
a conveyer belt of converted verts
ambitious girls enslaved by an expert.

The Book Of Armour

Newbies are fooled, queens fall
the kings of the cocks built a world to drill, hammer and screw a pining hole.
Working in a café at the south of the river
an Aesthetic Girl goes back to an ordinary figure
pouring pinots with sour lemons
the life she once knew has gone round full circle
she felt as if she'd never moved
the only difference now was a different front window view.
Looking out a miserable graffiti gloom
a Rolls Royce of a time
a big dipper she hoped would do loopily loop.

Her youthful skin had loosened and so did her grip
what kept her sadness away now became a septic pussing fib.
Her lip flipped, her Brazilian butt dipped
nature gave up, keeping it at bay,
her dreamy ways lived in a past tense of yesterday.
She was old newspaper, a gossip mag
A Chinese whisper
A teen's top shelf pornographic rag,
once Cashmere now just a slag.
Age wasn't on her side, memories now parked in the port of today
she tries covering up her cracks with a new perfume spray called, of the modern day.
She hoped new makeup would hide deaths verdict to be damned
but she's starting to realise, she's too late
her feet start to slip beneath her,
a funeral sitting on quicksand
built and rigged by many piglets employed to gold dig.
A dentist she called upon to help her with the teething, rotten with decay
her enamel abraded, toothless and shamed.

The Book Of Armour

Bright and orange, the distant infinity of a black matter of courage,
Soothing and cruising a poor life she found amusing but unfortunately karma found her actions disapproving,
everything to her, now felt so unamusing and tame.
Her Rome was smashed down it only took a day
beggars can't be choosers when lives are left in the hands of the self-made.
The innocent are turned and pulled towards one way
it's all a distraction to not remember the end goal is where we all came.

She couldn't feel anything anymore,
for shame, for shame
she didn't feel no more but O' if she did
her wishes would be to spawn,
a button she wished she could press to restart.
A desire for her pointless life to continue so that one day her prayers will be answered
a new quest a new request a truth in gest,
a superstition won her a lottery ticket, a pull on the wheel of fortune.
Full moons at night, wishing upon shooting stars
a bigger scope was needed to reach and park on planet Mars,
she undone Orion's belt that was her first mistake
she should of passed
she needed to turn back and leave the rocket where it was.
She scrambled around, a shoe size too big,
for her feet don't fit in The Materials Man's plan.
She learnt the hard way, authentic and nude
her coloured nails now firmly walk with a thudding mood.

The Book Of Armour

A pinball rebounded, her life is not so safe and sound
a baptism of fire, a turntable, a change of direction,
a wind unpredictably wild
she wants a spelling check in New Times Roman, casted in copper and iron,
a longing for a dissolvent.
She whisks up a witch's remedy for the ability to go back to an adolescent stage
a dreamy yearn to lay in a bathtub washing herself back at the orphanage.
A clover leaf
a butterfly on a lead
she walks around ladders that stand up further, than what she can foresee
every person that walks past her shadow can here the eerie murmured words,
of a regretful misdemeanor.

For now it's too late, this night owl met too many worms soiling her soul
survivors are the early birds who will always be the first up at dawn,
Sanity is only born once but this girl will die twice
But yet, she still flails to keep the quality of a suffice.

Aesthetic Girls are moldy and cut so deeply
a cheese caught up in strings by the grater of life
knives out and sharpened, a board to entice,
it's what they call visual merchandise.
A slot was ready to be coined
to leave her past behind
she risked it all for a gourmet life,
but only given a smidgen
a taster, a chice.

The Book Of Armour

Millions stifled, blind mice shuffled
she was trapped in a hamster ball, she relied on the machine
she was starry eyed, it was pinging her around
pinballed and dizzy she was everyone's rebound.
All to gain leverage to new solid ground
back yet again but beaten back down,
scorned and defiant a woman's superpower is resilient and final
a pretty rose thorned and out of soil,
she swings and stems to where she can find vitamin D
begging to be picked up and taken to the start
where she walked the streets, of eggshell town.

She believed she could get to a safe place
somehow her fragility still hid from bachelor hounds
now she's forbidden, an outcast that's powerless to arouse
barred and not forgiven a vulnerable girl in need of a hand.

An illusion of a money tree in need of an olive branch,
a sunflower of dreams
she fell from a great height
a treacle dart
that missed the bullseye,
the longer she hid the more pain in her suffering
a deterioration of a blanket that was far too smothering.
She rolled and rolled to discover
but frustratingly in the end
she took her bruises and battering
a forcefield she did not see,
for a life that flattered to deceive.

She looked down and saw four legs that held her in stead
the penny dropped
she caught the truth like a virus, her iris widened as her mind whispered…
'surplusss to requirementsssss'.
Suicidal as she starts to see straight
emotion is a poison she tried to tip away
from her heart, arteries and the mains,
unplugged, her light has been turned off
but an update of her senses had come back to life.

She knew a personality doesn't get a man into bed
she asked herself a question which said,
"Have I always been misled?"
"Should I of let my heart overrule my head?"
Everything reminded her of colours of red
hazardous danger, obsessed with the safety net,
she dreaded to think, where she stepped
it was a place she wouldn't of dreamt that she crept.

The outer self was her comfort zone
it was her only way to dwell,
it protected her for when she fell
a rolling ball with a fortune to tell
it repeatedly sold her a peaceful life
in the hope it would overwhelm.

After her buttered years of numbness,
she was mystified by what she'd become
pulled left and right, brought up and let down
smackdown, knocked out.

Now she sees the wood from the trees
once a Schmidt,
a hypocrite
just a hummingbird winging it.
A turbulent life which ended in a heavy landing
she flew the best she could
but in truth she crashed before radar could signal, that she was screwed.
Her dignity gone, she just about kept her clothes on
it's a good job she never had a son,
God sent an epiphany from above
that told her that weakness is not a sin, actually
a savior, a next of kin.
An Aesthetic Girl that learnt the hard way
a humbling lesson, who was determined to be queen
she was a victim that fell short to a harsh reality
to choose to fight or to surrender in fright makes life unlivable,
balance is the key to life.

*It's unfortunate parring does not exist, we can only dream
so, before the ball runs away from you and me
your principles must be turned by the wheel.
As innocence commences an impossibility emerges, to heal
7 sins are concealed in you, don't let your soul be uncompromised from a bad ordeal.
So, the only way to escape a repeated reel is to feel comfortably fearful,
it's the only way to keep the power to feel.*

*Life is a torturous cycle we are continuous bait
people must accept we are all predators, and we are all prey.
Monsters do not cease she learnt this the hard way
Being a cowardice human, keeps peace running away.*

The Book Of Armour

THE RELIGIOUS MAN

A man without a prayer
born just to be sold
he was born with love but his faith a decode,
a hate language with an ability to mould.
Pleasure runs in fear encrypted, hidden behind rough skin.
He was camouflaged in his environment
Socialistic faculties got on top
just an ordinary man who didn't believe in a man called God.
A shoddy existential ideology
coming from a one world plan of lords and bots
rooted in earth, mixed in a pot
in life your given what you got.
You're chewing with gums, teething and stuck
filled with chemicals of poison muck.
The Religious Man used dental floss, he brushed and brushed
but no matter what we are mutated cattle in cuffs.
Elders traded,
Caesars of peace and sordid soldiers sheath
we took our words literal a back seat ride life under a cartel dome
one in 400 million
they call it luck
but O' how we discovered we fucked it up.
The Religious Man tried drugs, women, liquor and betting
wrapped with insecurity,
desperate and offsetting
trying to find something to believe in but his mind rented
an agent for sale and for letting.

The Book Of Armour

*He never really found his place, feet sinking in a dessert of quicksand
he always ended with egg on his face,
a yolk in the sky
he wondered why
it never went right
while others stay on track
he didn't realise he had 9 lives,
but if pigs could fly
he would fly away
jumping in front of a one-way train.
Delayed and undeveloped, stuttering with hesitation
there's a malfunction in his operation
the temptation was there for self-detonation.*

*He never was in control
never believed he was in the wrong
an emergency break, he couldn't pull to jump start and ignite his soul.*

*He never could grasp a hold
a sticky substance
a lack of skill
he found it impossible to master
always made a mill of it.
Life is defined by your craft
a marksman fencing
bow and arrow bending
life a blessing? Impending.
Another person that holds the key but the weather changes unexpectedly
sunbathing in wintery rays impulsively.*

The Book Of Armour

A man unarmoured found himself with a hair transplant
a gym membership to match, he worked aggressively to gain a six pack.

He studied hard and climbed to the top of the ladder
business trips outbound
he drove and took advantage in an Aston drop top
an addict to astound
his father was proud,
revving to impress each lady with a loud exhaust sound.
His livelihood grew shrapnel and flesh become one
with each character he breathed and blew his livelihood grew,
the line between shrapnel and flesh became invisible.
The swelling was disabling and layering
a pixilation of what he thought his heart was truly saying.
Two testicles running in rage from a past that dictated his next move
chasing to break from the misery of previous days
kept him on a path between straight and narrow lanes
he had no boundaries, no obstacles to a fickle way of life.
He replaced everything he sees
that could help fill a deep groove
people's compliments of approval,
cars, houses and jewels used as commodities
there was no mountain he couldn't move.
A moral sacrifice
an author of his own fictional story
a crucifixion prisoned by his own conviction,
he hoped would fill the void.

The Book Of Armour

As time was wasted, he took a step back
a prediction he forested
a cyclone of paranoia spiraled and pulled up trees
confused with what he should do
he kept looking for a truth, an iron maiden, a shelter, a roof
but nothing could do the job to open the gates of his chute.

A portfolio of pictures
black and white images of a past
poleaxed from his own booth.

Cocooned with his luxury goods
gold watches and Cuban cigars
adored by people that he never heard of,
behind his back they laughed and moaned.
A daft way to live but a man with armour is a man that will die on his shield
his will is demonic, diametrically brainwashed but he believed he was good.
Platonically improving his good blood weakened by a blood type,
an alphabetical sequence
he wrote his obituary from painful ink, an art attack
pain killers that shamed his name
now mentally ill by life's X-files.
A man living in denial
the gold pasted walls of a ward
that lives within his skin
an ingrown nail that now has outgrown him.
A man with no next of kin
his final hope was a biblical connection, a confession of all sins,
a decision to attach himself to a lifesaving machine.

The Book Of Armour

A bible landed on his lap, he turned a new page
it was black and white
bland, holy and beige.
Chapters and structure
a lesson to learn
a story to play, to not plan a future is foolishly insane.
The penny finally dropped a new man enlightened by a new hope
he learnt it's important to think ahead and not just for today,
for impulsive short-term serenades are inflamed to blow up like a grenade
to live in tomorrow land is the way to play the game.
Two faces cut by the shrapnel
your left with nothing to gain but a signal of pain
green people protected by a metal case
no longer bullet-proof amber to red
for no one stops a parcel that is subliminally passed on.

Human beings believe they can't do no wrong
pennies are caught
people are dropped
no love for anybody
human beings start with a full stop.
This magical book covered in fingerprints and dotted sins
under a family tree a lifetime of fibs,
they do not wish to wipe the slate clean
a first page of a chapter, people don't turn to live
they had chosen death, a slave to their atomical armoury.

The Book Of Armour

Now a Religious Man,
God his chosen armour baptised in his name
the final call,
the last opportunity,
his last chance saloon
before the curtain closes and subdues his mood.
A final sprint in a marathon race, he kills for triumphant affairs
a refusal to be second best.
A message withheld
years wasted peddling
a no man's land of gloom, his head told him that nice guys lose
angels playing harps but his heart was out of tune
in heaven notes are invisible, a nonprofitable value.

A man now a monster controlled by a creator
living peace, a life now spiritually serene in tranquility
his debt was finally paid off
a new life, free and uncollared from his master's leash and vice,
tactics of entice, abolished by the powerful lords might.
It's now water off a duck's back
he's thankful for the window of pain
thankful that God resurrected his blessings and allowed him to stay
time was of the essence,
as now he only has himself to blame.
One book and a concrete building is all it took
a moral way of living, built centuries ago
a man now not in the lost ark
a new path built from handwork
foundations from graft now dug deep and strong
to be sustainable, consistency always needs something to lay on.

Theoretical weak ideas caused by bulldozing minds
created from rotting fears and dampened by acid rainfalls
he felt to disconnect was the best way to power his nuclear supply.
A raw plug to stop a leakage
a valve that couldn't stop to seep
tepid actions, an act to siege.
A plague too impactful to cast doubt
it was a betrayal of one's ego to gain clout
but now a man as good as new
a man with an appreciation of life
gift boxed and ribbons that tied and wrapped to cocoon.
A past life of hell, crossed off
he turned to symbolic psalms,
in remand, nailed but now free,
a defendant in waiting, he had a bad dream.

A man reborn and reset, now honest and reformed
he turned to teaching like his father blessed him to be,
he studied the art to preach, the wisdom from the armour of a priest,
he now fully believes in what his vocation is,
his prerogative has changed and so has his definition of what achievement means.
Nothing else to hide behind but the errors he made
that came by being a statistical number, born to a blind race.
He decided to abide to a religious set of rules
and with fine lines he worshipped a new way of life.
He turned himself back to front and inside out, a new shrine he decided to die for,
he's ready to be a guide, to lead the naive who were backstabbed by life.
For those whose hero's turned to villains of misery blues
a treaty designed for buskers and glamourous moguls.

The Book Of Armour

A life for the devoured
love is real but so hard to conquer
for once he felt positive energy from his elders.
the words that were once Greek
now a meaning, he could finally read.
A scripture unearthed from the year of A.D.
The hardship of life that fatigued
no longer covered him in sheets of shame
he felt a glow above his head
he washed it down a new passageway,
a redefining new direction came, from what he left astray.
He now has the minerals
the natural ingredients to serve a Sunday service,
an interjected past with a holistic ray
negative kryptonite
stopped by the ozone haze.

He is the teacher that got taught
a pupil that had to learn again
he unlearnt and gave back what he didn't deserve to earn.
Life is the head
it got him by the neck
a boy to a God
for the sake of the greater good,
for years he hid under a hood
to possess what he always had in which only time and his heart understood.
The dog controlled and lock jawed, he shot for the stars and a caught a wish bone
flexing his muscles, it was all for show.

He was first in line, an arsenal was spurred by a man from dirt
a homing missile backfired
a tank deterrent
a war which started from a man of dust
now seals of sirs insecure from the unjust.

Hysteria for other colonies
militant to get his 6 pence
a pocket full of change
but no way a soldier could ever change their ways.
A suicide bomber attached to a switch
a trigger button of red rage
a man searching for something he never found, it was all so vague.
It changed daily depending on the exchange rate,
extremities of mother nature, hurricanes and tirades
you must pay for a ticket to win it, there's no two ways.
No way out
the only way is to go deeper underground and under the skin
noise cancelling alarms and mass compounds,
brothers and sisters in arms, unfortunately this is a dream too far.
People are always running away to see better days
it's impossible for them to stay calm, their biggest fear is in their own skeleton.
Selectors of what they declare
guns at the ready while others shoot flairs
but they say it's just hot smoke, swept up aimlessly in the air.

The Book Of Armour

A paradoxical tear
it's clear to see, we all crave the care,
rooted from baby food
fed by aging clones
who wouldn't and in some cases, couldn't help the next generation's brittle bones,
but for the elite 1% they travel faster than what we can compute
a constructed hardware built to pull down the 99 percentiles pursuit.

50 years later this survivor turned to The Lord's Prayer
for this child of God hasn't looked back,
he stares in the mirror but sees the same red glare
as he tries not to drift, for armour is a trap he now fears.
He sold his soul to the devil
so the beating would stop
his morals were crossed
his sins were underlined
his excuse is that "every human had signed to the bind."
Behind each life a wall is written on, from trauma from a past life
but nobody minds the victims they kill on their way
far too focused on 6 seconds of happiness,
it's all there is,
it's black and white,
it's all they provide,
an epiphany to heal he thought there was no downside.

Till one day he fell back down to earth on his own shield
there was only one thing left to do and that was to scream help
so, he kneeled on one leg
he took it all on board,
a new philosophy, to break away from a 10-tonne kettlebell.

The Book Of Armour

A broken man now gained the ability to walk into heaven and away from hell,
he unlocked its gates
life isn't something smitten filled with cuddly kittens
on the contrary, people are frightened and bitten.
As people deliberate their own demise
perished unfairly but life doesn't care
people are left naked our love is scarce,
life's a bitch but the bastard in us all must play its part to fit.
It only took him to fall from grace to understand he lost what he couldn't replace,
a contract signed by Crowley's prophesy
nothing to separate the arts of blackened arteries,
a hand held out from the Manson family.

With a handshake and word as strong as oak,
a token to the afterlife
he was schooled by the prophets as God enjoyed the show
After, he sent a revelation for him to change but to no ovation
for a man is an ox, a stubborn lover of confrontation.

He calls you John the most deranged and wrong
but yet for his most beloved he forgives, but what does he really think?
Smirking behind a face mask, a man's casket, an old dear
a fate generously given then thumped, he does it for a career.
We are copycats, copyright by design
we scavenge around, then blame the rats
the only difference is a man is hard to catch.

The Book Of Armour

A natural filter to sieve
a man's life is over before he can blink
God doesn't miss a thing
life is short and bleak
but we are supposed to remember, he's done us all a big old favour.

A farmer of given fate
everyone's on a probational slaughter,
we wait, we wait…

It's better for living things to die in their sleep
it helps the dead not to weep
The Aesthetic Girl's mother had no money for a lifesaving treat.
Her daughter was losing fast
her mother's broken, covered in cast
her armour disintegrating week by week
due to her deteriorating health, a religious man she seeked.
Her armour and dignity broken and burned on a fragile stave
she stumbled, crumbling from each loose stone that was paved
once a dame, now the same as the drunk on Penny Lane.
She walked and walked till she found her nearest church
she was willing to be the next unarmed convert.

Slugging through
walking the concrete dessert
too deep into murky muddy waters,
she went too far to turn back
she sees the stain glass windows
a man with a cross on his back
life was white but for this old lady completely black.

The Book Of Armour

Now a pervert of colour had emerged
determined to live and a will to be reborn
she gazes with eyes wide, a hope to a new devine,
like a baby sucking its mother's breast for the very first time.
She smelt the truth as it misted beneath the large steel doors
she entered fragilely, her bones clicking as she walked along the mosaic floor
but the high ceilings above kept her believing her death sentence meant more.

A statue of Christ roamed around her head of torment
looking down at a mother with meds
she breaks down in front of the priest, his patience she would test
to her astonishment he held a hand out; he was ready to break bread.
She prayed to The Religious Man as she cried for help
the choir in the background angelically whelped
the unarmoured victim let it all out
a repent of sins nobody could help
"I abandoned my child." She wept,
fast forward 50 years a habit she passed to herself,
hopes of being able to overcome
but bad habits are not born but learnt
she pleads and begs but her vulnerability is now lost and dead
now resurrected by a grim reaper crossing hairs.
The Religious Man snared, sympathised then said,

"An incurable fate is in your hands not in the eyes of the blind
each armoured victim eventually resigns,
denialism comes from a box you all designed
your admittance in confession,
your arrears are owed,
you kept them hidden,

The Book Of Armour

*for you reconciled to defeat
by the truth that you decided to keep forbidden."
The Religious Man gave his words in grace
those words were to follow God's ways
he continued to speak and say,*

*"Be truthful and learn from your adolescent stage
your fate was created by incurable hoorays,
as time has now caught up, there is no hiding place,
armoured people do not care they silently live in a place of despair,
as life for us all, is too much to bare."
"Different characters geared up to fight
warriors burrowed with tunnel visioned sight
Skeletons of a build, your motives were concealed
you cut your nose off
for it was an easier road than to peel.*

*I see all hearts hiding behind their shields
between me and you
just to list a few;*

*A Status Man at 74 now suffering from loneliness
an agoraphobe with no one to console.
Once a wife now deceased, the love she didn't get was her only need
A Material Man's business liquidated by default
An Aesthetic Girl now a crack addict and poor
and last but not least, a mother's home is now a hospital."*

The Religious Man goes on to say…

The Book Of Armour

"Different armoured caricatures are dented in the end
but armour helps you to get through the painful dread,
for the people too weak that rely on honest beats
survival for us all is dependent on more than one living thing."

"Acute deceitfulness that lives in us all
we live on the edge of a triangle
we are equilaterally flawed
we bicker scratch and claw
we are fighting ourselves we are Gods of war.
Every one of us are born weak with no armour at all
our weapons are birthed by what's decomposed
but we join an alliance to silence our woes,
our comprehension needs to improve for us to be composed.
We must come together and suspend ourselves
from running a race checkered in melancholy.
A false start and a white flag from the first second
children are given a bad hand,
perspective and lessons, an adult book written by an adolescent mind.
The key is held by the pure,
deaf and blind infants hold the difference
they defend and cope immaculately
their strength is tenfold
they shield themselves by the love and laughter that flows,
honest to themselves, there is no bravado".

The Religious Man goes on to say…

*"They show there's no need for armour of ammunition to load,
persona and to pose leads to an adult being exposed,
adults only learn in time…
The character they are constrained to is an impossible pursue to obtain
it melts away then becomes an avalanche too heavy to tow."*

*The very ill mother teared up with guilt and shame,
but he continued and proceeded to say;*

*"You made a brave decision
to finally point the finger of blame onto your chest plate
you heroically took full responsibility
whether you live or die, you are now cleansed in God's eyes."*

*"An infection of lice
it jumps from ice to ice
every new life is knitted by the ones who carry bad goods of supply,
it's impossible to eradicate and cure
so an armour is our compromise.
"I wish somehow children could prepare
if only people were two steps ahead
time wouldn't need to intervene and repair,
for now, its damage limitation
the entirety of love we cannot share."*

The Book Of Armour

The Mother recognised there was no hope
The Religious Man's words didn't break, it just peddled through the gears
what she really needed was a time machine to reverse,
it started to sink in that fairy tale stories don't finish first

She suddenly came to terms that the last page ends in a hirst.
Following or leading it doesn't really matter
billions of people shattered
a paradise as toxic as diesel.
She just wants to go now
she's fed up with the upheaval,
life is a rocky mountain that's steep and evil.

Bitterness from discovery
she knows she fucked up
she lived her life corrupt
she relied and preyed on the armoured ones,
swarming down like a vulture that smells blood
she fed on the able body of a paralysed mind, a dud.
The convocation died and so did her belief
that The Religious Man could ever get her back on her feet.
With despondency and tormented serenity
she heard the familiar sound of a pair of Louboutin heels
she looked around in curiosity,
she sees her daughter in season old designer clothes
this time with no persona, or pouty pose.

The Book Of Armour

Just a coat hanger and a come down from her last dose
she saw the cracks it appeared in her veins
tear ducks worked that brick layers paved,
a fantasy coshed
a cause of substance, hazardous to health.

She walked on by,
right past her mother's crying eyes
The Aesthetic Girl concedes and kisses The Religious Man's feet,
her mother was speechless in defeat.
Fate had played a part
the keepers were finders of the punishers of greed
it was like a movie, the mother had front row seats.
Holy priests and angel choirs brought the heat,
She had her red wine poured money given up to a charitable law
as The Aesthetic Girl was manifesting the power for her fortunes to bring change
The Religious Man begrudgingly had to explain his wisdom all again.
The same reaction occurred for a second time
her hopes, a murdered trend
as that of her mauled, tatted fur coat,
profanity is the pronunciation of death.

The Aesthetic Girl smelled something familiar
burnt by a burning wood fire
she gets off the floor by The Religious Man's leather laced clogs
she stands up in disbelief and quickly tries to hide her face,
her mind's a fog.

The Book Of Armour

A revengeful bitter ex-wife's face that told a thousand sleepless nights on the rocks
negative minded she hoped the people she blamed would get their comeuppance
she looked behind towards the entrance,
astonished and bemused she was shocked by what her light and eyes fused.
She cracked a smile it didn't wait, it pushed its way to the front of the queue.

The Material Man had raised his ugly head
the newly wed memories now just a Wednesday to forget
every footstep he trod the closer he got; the more ash lunged from his clutch.
Walking in rags the man sold everything he had
once pulled by horsepower now he relies on instincts of the animal kingdom
an expensive price for a crucified pride
a symbolic image, an anti-Christ.

A renaissance he trusts
as he's a man that is used to winning,
the word losing, he doesn't believe in, he calls it fly tipping.
He knows he's lost the battle but defiantly babbles
"I will win the war." He calls, but no one answers.
Like a dog in a lake helplessly paddling
The Religious Man finds it amusing watching him rambling, scrambling, cackling.
A delusional man kept shooting words to sooth
a charismatic sentence he states, "This is just the start."

The Book Of Armour

An arrogant man is hard to stand,
boring and bland he stands before the man who's seen it all before
5 days and hours of 24.
Back handed compliments and threats of a rat a tat tat
for The Religious Man hes a 7th dam
he turns defences into attack and attack to defence
desperate unarmoured bats come out only when blind, dark and dense.
For Gods naive children
the tables have now turned
a tortoise thrown from front to back
a shell too heavy to call a home.
The Religious Man dressed in robes with patience to help the uneducated
sufferers, throwing stones
anyhow he vowed to go on, more wise words had come and gone.

He could relate and appreciate although he never told the secrets of his past,
he didn't allow it to blab out
Like the troubles of the broken who come to him and ask for help,
it was his way of giving back to himself.

The Religious Man knew he was lucky
for the late choices he made
he managed to get away with it by the skin of his teeth
memories never really fade.

It wasn't easy for him to escape for life came at him fast
it's so easy to snap and break
life's an anaconda that subdues its prey
constricting a construct everyone must obey.

*A character everyone must make to secure a person more time
before an inevitable plague.
Bones are biological the truth is in our DNA
we are not a conceptual plastic model put up on display.*

*The Religious Man finished his final sentence
The Material Man sat next to a mother-in-law he once called his,
they cried into each other's embrace,
what was missing has now been replaced.*

*The Aesthetic Girl had glanced over, she had an epiphany
she quickly realised something she found so strange,
she couldn't bring herself to say it
but under her breath she silently conveyed
the sentence of 5 words, "We are all the same."*

*All differences were instantly erased
between 3 victims cursed by tainted birthdays
united and together for the first time
now filled with pride, haters turned to supporters,
their hate declined, bodied and died.
enlightenment shined down
spotlight from above
a compass circled an outline of trust.*

*The heavy shoulders that were once weighing them down
are now 6 feet above and firmly on the ground.
The Religious Man blessed them with holy water
then went on to say one last prayer
then filed them all for divorce from their luciferian guardian care.*

The Book Of Armour

An exorcism to open what was concealed
Satan was shown the exit
a son of God's, revealed,
Now more a funeral director than a priest
An entrance to an exit strategy.
Funny how things turn upside down
impossible to reverse you can only go forward,
People don't realise
life has a game in hand.
It's a small world after all
what goes around comes around
what goes up must eventually come down.

A slinky spring loaded with no way to reload,
all you can do is sit back and watch as random events occur;
if you're lucky you'll avoid the feds
if you're lucky you'll avoid the meds
if you're lucky you won't let the insanity take over your head
if you're lucky you'll be able to pick yourself up to get out of bed
if you're lucky, you'll be lucky
for life goes on…
It just goes on…
Whether you perform or it turns out to be a false storm
it's our intelligence that steals the pleasures of tomorrow show
we are the clowns in a performance managed by the CEO's.

It's not your fault how you faired
your born and bred dependent on a matching pair
you're here because a slut opened her legs and shared her eggs
fertilised by a cockroach with needs, an objective in which he achieved.

The Book Of Armour

The cat gets the cream
only a child's happiness spoiled, a generous offer that was coffered,
when things get wet, a father of secrecy tends to forget
nobody benefits except a man running in fear of his debt.
So people polish and window clean
everything on the outside is full of beauty
we all neglect what we once ran to fetch
it's a pity we don't stop till our unrealistic expectations are met.

The Religious Man is all but done
he's about to round up his lecture and put away his gun,
a holster to safeguard to keep moving forward
a reminder that his armour is just as heavy as yours.
He carries every regretful action on his bareback
the truth is a responsibility, it takes unimaginable courage and strength.
This man's armour is not to hide but to seek
he has chosen to be a shield for the weak.
He decided to sacrifice himself and lift others up
we must choose
an armour, a caricature, a seesaw affect,
we clearly must live to die with regret.

We rely on our designer status
the money we heist
it keeps people tied we turn our noses up, at the mundane collared 9-5's.
But this causes misery to actors and to the ones that lose their way
So let's try to mend what has now been done,
we need to stop this fearful notion to run.

The Book Of Armour

Support a fool with an armoured shell
it's only a coping mechanism to protect what we dwell
life is a disaster for many it's hell,
we cover up our grazes with the laughs and joy we tell.

We create a character to write a story
a show case title named, "we are doing well".
We all compete the winner retrieves a prize of self-esteem,
for what people fight against is a guilty feeling.

Everyone's walls are theirs to protect the cracks that are plastered
8 layered slaves to 1 puppet master
we all find life hard and we all find ways to adapt
people need to encourage others, not to give them flack.

After the spats and fights
lessons are taught to be kind
support everyone
as everyone is flawed,
a handicap of foresight.

The armour we carry
a shield and a sword
as we attack each other and as we defend,
we all have one thing in common
a desperate plea to mend.

People must unite to plaster their wounds
otherwise the chickens come home,
they come home to roost.

The Book Of Armour

People of fragility weakened by genuine victims of humility,
they fall to unhealth
too numb to change
they beg the people with strength to alter their fate.
The armoured and strong carry on enjoying the fruits of their labor
they ignore and carry on and sing their own songs
using the minds of the naive and young,
until the indefensible, no longer can hang on.

The despicable and the abused addicts are skewed
lost minds with internal feuds,
emotional logs thrown into the fire to fume
burnt ashes scattered to groom
sympathy isn't given
it goes against the brood of the new.

No strength to hold
an armour dependent on knights of metal
but armoured people do not care they leave the unequipped in despair,
for life is already too much for everyone to bare.
Different characters chosen to fight
warriors with tunnel visioned sight
using each other as a source of light,
motives concealed an army built of skeletons that led
means there's always going to be an increase of horrific bloodshed.

So we owe our stories for the ones who will never know
the pain and struggle the war we condone
let's take off our suits, we are not bullet proof, just sensitive people,
a family who lives under the same roof.

The Book Of Armour

THE
HARDSHIP
Of
LIFE

THE HARDSHIP OF LIFE

Teacher's parents desire to instill infants with catchy headlines
"You have character." Is the appeal,
but it takes a ghost to ask, "What is your character?"
They choose our creed, our beliefs, our name and our means,
they forget to tell you your life depends on where the pendulum swings,
they forget to tell you this is as easy as it gets
the odds outside are not in favour of your bets,
the harsh reality is coming…
The harsh reality is coming…
Day by day,
month by month,
year by year,
growing up, sand pits soon become a thing of the past.
We choose to trade computers
smart phones
cars and beautiful homes, in exchange to starve.

We learnt what our elders told us
until we get much older and regret in somber,
O' we did anything to become what we were told,
so they couldn't say, "I told you!"
So, we created and chose a way to deflect the responsibility every day
but the truth was there at the beginning
it was staring us in the face.

*People with character
role models strong and solid,
innocence removed robotic from blues
elegantly mistaken designed to misuse.
But there's not a bad word I can say
a man must do what he needs to do
how can you be mad?
When everyone hadn't a choice but to choose to not be sad.
It's the only way to get through
unfortunately, we all breathe O_2
the dead cry for our strife
they call it:*

"The Hardship Of Life."

*Childish dreams and sensitive minds
to which have died,
heavy hearts now living a lie
innocent eyes wiped
backed into a corner a character to find,
threw away the dice he followed and shiest
preyed on people and blamed on a vice
abandoning their instincts including Christ.*

*It was the only way for them to get through
the dead cry for our strife,
they call it:*

"The Hardship Of Life".

*Many cried at the hands of a man with a personality that draws up a plan
to rub out where it all began.
Time is his shrine
people pied
money given the rights for him to hide.
A fragile calculator
a warmed perception engineered from a delusional traumatized mind.
It stems and continues, its rife
its called:*

"The Hardship Of Life."

*His purse is empty from morals of debt
for its easier to forget that pieces of himself have now been spent,
a meaning of life is now survival of rent.
economics aside everyone has their fingers in the pie,
it's called:*

"The Hardship Of Life."

*Little do we learn people grow up way to firm
turn their selves into characters they try and own to keep their truth inside,
to hide behind*

"The Hardship Of Life."

*Everyone must choose a character that coincides with their ego
that sides with the dreams that live within
we wish we could be the things we had since we were 3.*

An impossibility to restore
we are pushed up against the wall
pupils dry,
flesh mauled and broken
we never learn,
we are on our knees yet again crawling in testimony.

A character chosen by us all,
erosion to implosion
a devil's potion
it gives us motion.
For life is not worth living but for money,
religion, status and treasures of aesthetic
on the mind, broken inside
creates an armour for our tissues to hide.
Let's pray and be kind
we don't want a dimming of lights
as we all should support each other's lies
as we all have one thing in common
it's called:

"The Hardship Of Life."

So we should all count our blessings to the penny
as each man and woman is a slave to the money
a reason to stop the misery we're ignoring
to further ourselves for what we know by withdrawing
a value we'll never realise we already owned
the matrix believes innocence is weakness
a ritual of organisation and neatness.

We use protection
God's our witness
a choice of ill health or a choice of sickness.

Printed in Poland
by Amazon Fulfillment
Poland Sp. z o.o., Wrocław
15 October 2022

8aec3c89-b5c9-4e36-bb9b-8da2d86b3982R01